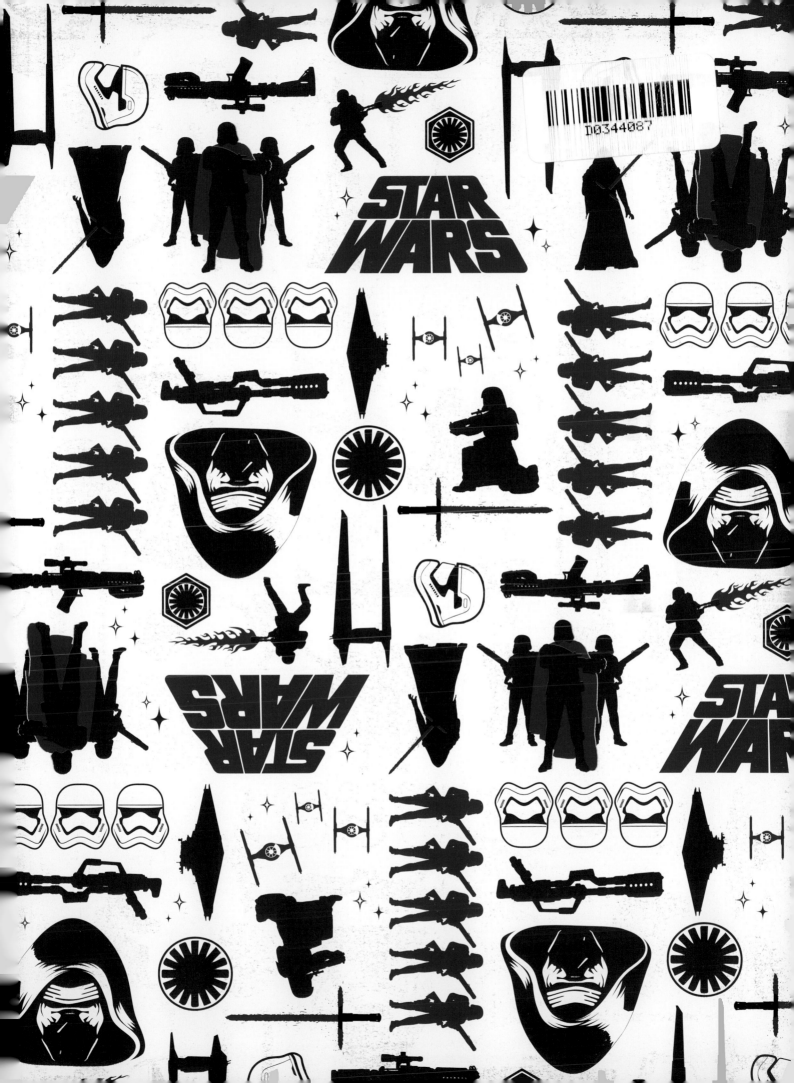

EGMONT
We bring stories to life

First published in Great Britain 2016 by Egmont UK Limited
The Yellow Building, 1 Nicholas Road, London W11 4AN

Cover illustration by Adi Granov
Written by Frank Tennyson
Designed by Richie Hull, Glen Downey and John Stuckey

© & ™ 2016 Lucasfilm Ltd.

ISBN 978 1 4052 8347 2

63783/1

Printed in Italy

To find more great *Star Wars* books, visit www.egmont.co.uk/starwars

WELCOME

Welcome back to a galaxy far, far away! Visit strange worlds, discover alien creatures, and meet new heroes and villains along the way.

We'll travel from the harsh deserts of Jakku to the frozen forests of Starkiller Base, discover the dark secrets of the sinister Kylo Ren, and blast off for adventure in the famous *Millennium Falcon* once more.

Enter your name, species and home world to begin ...

NAME

SPECIES

HOME WORLD

CONTENTS

THE STORY SO FAR

A whistle-stop tour of *The Force Awakens*

THE FIRST ORDER

Thirty years after the defeat of the Empire a new menace emerges. The evil First Order aim to eliminate the last remaining Jedi and the Resistance.

MEET KYLO REN

The First Order's terrifying enforcer is Kylo Ren, the son of Han Solo and Leia Organa. Originally trained by Luke Skywalker, he turns to the dark side and vows to destroy his missing uncle and everything the Jedi represent.

ALL-ACTION ESCAPE

Resistance pilot Poe Dameron obtains a map that reveals Luke's location and hides it in his astromech droid BB-8. After being captured and tortured by Kylo Ren, Poe escapes with the help of reformed stormtrooper Finn and they crash a stolen TIE fighter on the planet Jakku.

A NEW GENERATION

Separated from Poe at the crash site, Finn meets a hardened scavenger called Rey, who has already befriended BB-8. The First Order tracks them down and they make a daring escape on the *Millennium Falcon*.

THE ULTIMATE WEAPON

In Maz Kanata's castle, Rey stumbles across Luke's old lightsaber and after experiencing disturbing visions, flees into the woods. The First Order uses the Starkiller, a planet converted into a super weapon, to obliterate the Republic capital. They also launch an attack on Takodana to capture BB-8.

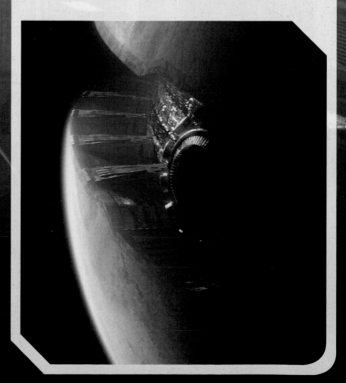

THE HEROES RETURN

The *Millennium Falcon* breaks down and is boarded by Han Solo and Chewbacca. On board, the *Falcon*'s crew view BB-8's map and realise it is incomplete. They travel to the planet Takodana to meet Resistance contact Maz Kanata.

A DARK ORDEAL

Kylo Ren captures Rey and takes her back to Starkiller Base for interrogation. Rey learns she can use the Force to resist his mind-reading abilities, and later escapes from her cell using a Jedi mind trick.

THE MASTER PLAN

The Resistance gathers at their HQ on D'Qar to plot the destruction of the Starkiller Base. Han, Chewbacca and Finn pilot the *Falcon* onto the base, disable its shields and plant explosives. They find Rey but unfortunately, they also cross paths with the vengeful Kylo Ren.

DEATH OF A LEGEND

Han promises Leia that he will try to return their son alive, but when the two meet it ends in disaster. Kylo Ren kills his father with a lightsaber blow.

KYLO REN MEETS HIS MATCH

After the explosives detonate and the X-wings attack, the base is destroyed. Before the planet implodes, Finn fights Kylo Ren in a lightsaber duel. He is badly wounded, so Rey steps in and overpowers the villain. Separated by a ravine, both parties escape the doomed planet.

RETURN OF THE JEDI

Back at the Resistance base, R2-D2 awakens from his hibernation and reveals his data banks contain enough information to complete BB-8's map. Luke's location is revealed and Rey, alongside Chewie and R2-D2, track him down to an island on a distant planet. Rey presents Luke with his lightsaber, starting a new chapter in the *Star Wars* saga.

THE GREAT ESCAPE

Han, Rey and Finn must make it to the *Millennium Falcon* before they are captured by criminal gangs. Help them through the maze while avoiding the rathtars along the way!

REY

FINN

HAN **START**

FINISH

SECRET WEAPON

The First Order is working on a weapon to rival the terrifying Death Star. Cross out every other letter to reveal the name of this deadly battle station.

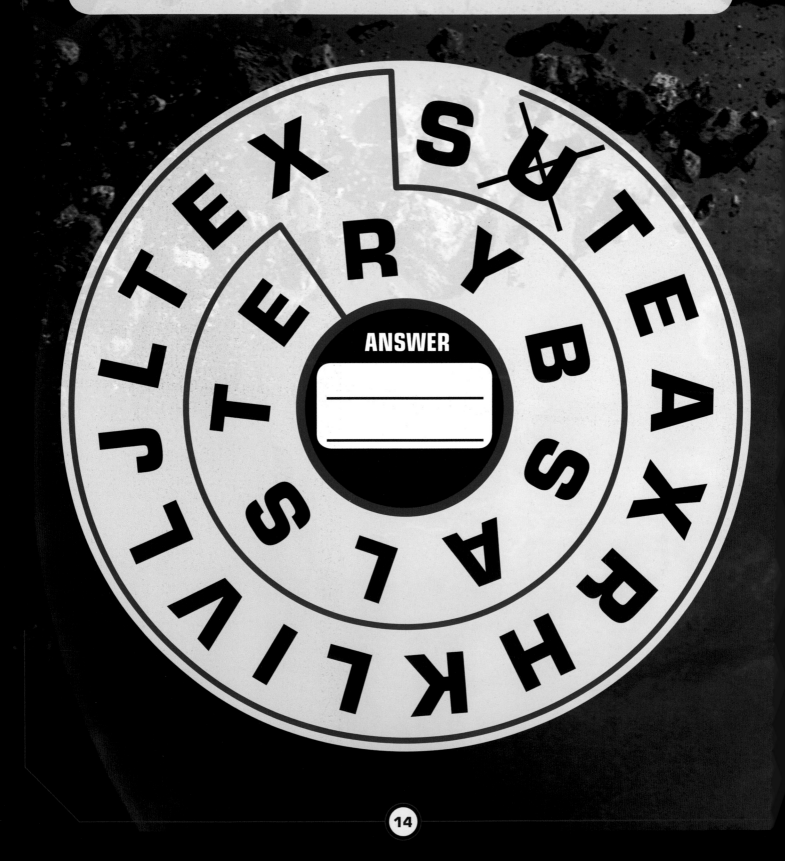

ANSWER

_ _ _ _ _ _ _

DRAW KYLO REN

Put your artistic powers to the test by drawing and colouring in *The Force Awakens'* villain.

DID YOU KNOW?

Kylo Ren is a member of the First Order, a military and political organisation committed to bringing back the "stability" that existed under the Empire. Ruled by Supreme Leader Snoke, the First Order plot to restore the glory of old.

WHO ARE YOU?

Where would you fit into the *Star Wars* story?
Take this quiz to find out!

QUESTIONS	A	B	C
1 You hear old stories about Jedi and their daring deeds. What do you do?	Ask to hear more. The legend of the Jedi has always been fascinating. ☐	Look on with bafflement. You were trained to fight, not listen to fairy tales. ☐	Explode in fury. The Jedi are a plague who need to be erased from the galaxy. ☐
2 The ship on which you are travelling develops a problem with its hyperdrive. What do you do?	Leap into action. You've spent your whole life fixing space junk. ☐	Try to help but, to be honest, you don't know the difference between a screwdriver and a Harris wrench. ☐	Instruct a minion to complete the repairs QUICKLY! Your temper tantrum has caused the damage. ☐
3 Supreme Leader Snoke wants to rule the galaxy. What do you think?	This guy is obviously a force for evil but I need to return home and wait for my family. ☐	No good can come from this so I want to get as far away from his influence as possible. ☐	Under Snoke's guidance I will bring back the great days of the Empire. ☐
4 Confronted by a ferocious rathtar what do you do?	I'll use my intelligence and find an ingenious way to trap the monster. ☐	I'm always up for a fight but sometimes you have to retreat when the odds are stacked against you. ☐	I cannot be defeated. This vile creature will fall at my knees. ☐
5 What do you think of droids?	They are quite valuable so they could make for a good trade. ☐	Droids are great in helping soldiers win battles. ☐	They are nothing but simple machines to serve the most powerful. ☐
6 Lightsabers are the ultimate weapon. Do you agree?	I don't know why, but there's something about lightsabers that make me uneasy. ☐	A weapon is just a weapon, isn't it? ☐	A lightsaber is a symbol of great power. ☐
7 What does the Force mean to you?	Something scary but I'm willing to learn how to use it. ☐	To be honest, I have no idea how it works. ☐	The ability to get what I want, when I want. ☐

MOSTLY A

You are clever and resourceful. The Force is truly with you.

You are most like REY

MOSTLY B

You are courageous and practical. You are a good ally in a fight.

You are most like FINN

MOSTLY C

The dark side is strong in you. You don't let anyone stand in your way.

You are most like KYLO REN

TOP FACTS
KYLO REN

Everything you need to know about the Master of the Knights of Ren

FAMOUS PARENTS

Kylo Ren, born "Ben", is son of Princess Leia and Han Solo. Following in the footsteps of his grandfather, Anakin Skywalker, Kylo Ren turns away from his parents to the dark side.

JEDI IN TRAINING

He trains with his uncle, Luke Skywalker, but this ends in disaster as he falls under the spell of the evil Supreme Leader Snoke. After killing the next generation of Jedi, Ben takes the name Kylo Ren and serves the First Order.

THE GHOST OF VADER

Kylo is obsessed with the deeds of Darth Vader, dressing in similar attire and even speaking to Vader's ruined helmet for advice.

MAN ON A MISSION

Kylo Ren dedicates his life to destroying the last remaining Jedi. The quest to hunt down Luke Skywalker consumes his every waking hour.

THE POWER WITHIN

Master of the Knights of Ren, he has incredible Force powers, including the ability to control minds, inflict physical and mental pain, and send opponents flying through the air. He can even suspend a blaster bolt with a single thought.

THE CALL TO THE LIGHT

Although an evil villain guilty of murdering countless innocents, Kylo Ren is tortured by thoughts of good. Only by killing his father Han Solo can he banish "the call to the light".

AN ANGRY YOUNG MAN

When Kylo Ren receives bad news he is capable of astonishing violent rages, attacking his surroundings with his lightsaber and threatening anyone nearby.

THERE'S MORE TO COME

Although Kylo Ren is defeated by Rey, it is clear that Supreme Leader Snoke has further plans for his star pupil, and promises to complete his training.

THE IMPERFECT WEAPON

Ren's crudely built red lightsaber features a cracked kyber crystal, which can barely contain the weapon's power. The trademark cross guard is required to vent excess energy.

NEW ALIENS

Meet the weird and wonderful creatures from *The Force Awakens*

UNKAR PLUTT

Unkar Plutt is a junk boss on the planet Jakku, who rules his territory with an iron fist. He hires thugs to ensure that scavengers like Rey play by his rules, and offers only tiny amounts of survival rations in exchange for ship parts. He is in possession of the *Millennium Falcon* until Finn, Rey and BB-8 use it to make their escape.

SPECIES: Crolute

MAZ KANATA

A pirate legend, over 1,000 years old, Maz Kanata has a strong connection to the Force and can tell what people are feeling just by looking into their eyes. She sets up a smugglers' haven on Takodana where she meets Rey and encourages her to embrace the Force.

SPECIES: Unknown

TEEDO

We first meet a Teedo prowling the wastes of Jakku upon its cybernetic pack animal called a luggabeast. This small reptilian creature captures BB-8 in Rey's territory. Rey frees the droid declaring: "That's just Teedo, he has no respect for anyone."

SPECIES: Teedo

THROMBA AND LAPARO

A partnership who had set up their business in the castle of Maz Kanata, Thromba and Laparo are crypto-surgeons who offer cosmetic procedures to criminals who want to change their appearance. Their lab is destroyed when the First Order attack Kanata's castle.

SPECIES: Frigosian

SARCO PLANK

This ageing scavenger, bounty hunter and tomb raider relocates to Jakku, most likely to evade the many enemies he has made over a long career. Once upon a time, on the planet Devaron, Plank even fought Luke Skywalker!

SPECIES: Melitto

ATHGAR HEECE

Heece, a bounty hunter, operates in the Niima outpost and is used to working on worlds with high atmospheric pressures and temperatures. A hose provides Heece with processed atmosphere, so Jakku actually feels quite pleasant to him.

SPECIES: Dybrinthe

RATHTAR

Rathtars are ferocious, tentacled creatures, with sharp teeth and an ability to consume almost anything. They hunt in packs and are famed for their role in the Trillia massacre. They bring disaster to Han Solo's freighter when, having escaped their holds, they kill most of Kanjiklub and the Guavian Death Gang. Finn nearly meets the same fate before being rescued by Rey.

SPECIES: Rathtar

TROOPER TROUBLE

Finn is ready to leave his stormtrooper days behind him. Find six differences between these two pictures of the former First Order soldier.

BB-8 SEARCH

Help BB-8 search for *The Force Awakens* words in this grid – they can run up, down, backwards or diagonally.

V	L	V	F	A	L	C	O	N	C	J	Q	M	C	H
Z	G	R	E	S	I	S	T	A	N	C	E	H	D	G
Y	L	E	Y	D	B	E	P	P	N	A	R	T	O	O
L	E	P	C	H	E	W	B	A	C	C	A	R	Y	G
E	I	U	G	L	D	O	M	G	K	J	K	E	J	M
F	A	B	M	R	F	L	I	Y	J	Y	R	G	K	A
G	O	L	K	A	H	K	L	A	N	H	X	Q	R	Z
N	R	I	M	Y	F	O	K	O	F	Q	N	U	A	K
N	G	C	K	R	R	K	G	O	P	V	M	K	Z	A
I	A	Z	U	E	U	S	X	T	I	X	P	X	D	N
F	N	S	N	O	R	E	M	A	D	E	O	P	H	A
D	A	U	N	K	A	R	P	L	U	T	T	G	H	T
T	K	G	D	I	Q	Z	O	L	O	S	N	A	H	A
H	C	B	Q	R	E	D	R	O	T	S	R	I	F	U
S	T	A	R	K	I	L	L	E	R	I	S	Q	K	V

POE DAMERON	**CHEWBACCA**	**FIRST ORDER**	**STARKILLER**
REY	**KYLO REN**	**JAKKU**	**FALCON**
FINN	**UNKAR PLUTT**	**LEIA ORGANA**	**MAZ KANATA**
HAN SOLO	**REPUBLIC**	**ARTOO**	**RESISTANCE**

TOP FACTS
REY

Everything you need to know about the new hero with a mysterious past

A LONELY CHILDHOOD

Rey was left on Jakku at an early age and manages to survive on her own scavenging from old battlefields and selling scrap for food. We never learn of her parents or why she thinks "they'll be back, one day."

THE DROID'S NOT FOR SALE

Although hardened by her tough upbringing, Rey shows she is loyal when Unkar Plutt offers to buy BB-8. He offers her much needed food for the droid, but Rey, having become quite fond of her companion, refuses.

A TALENTED PILOT

Despite never having flown the *Millennium Falcon* before, Rey manages to quickly master the ship in a thrilling dog fight against several TIE fighters. Her skilful piloting through the wreckage of a Star Destroyer – and some instinctive gunning by Finn – results in a fantastic getaway.

MECHANICAL GENIUS

The *Millennium Falcon* is about to be flooded with poisonous gas, but Rey acts quickly to fix it. Later, she impresses Han by fixing the hyperdrive, allowing them to continue their escape.

A VISION OF THE PAST

In Maz Kanata's castle on Takodana, Rey is drawn to a room containing Luke Skywalker's lightsaber. Upon touching it she has terrifying visions, with glimpses of the past and future. Maz says the weapon now belongs to Rey and that she should let the Force guide her.

RESISTING REN

Kylo Ren attempts to extract information from the captured Rey but fails as she instinctively pushes back at him with the Force. After an intense mental struggle Rey reads Kylo Ren's thoughts revealing his innermost fears: "You're afraid...that you will never be as strong as Darth Vader!"

HEAD-TO-HEAD

Rey takes on Kylo Ren in a lightsaber battle and is able to summon her weapon by using the Force. Just as Kylo Ren seems to gain the upper hand, she begins to draw on her new-found powers. Eventually Rey defeats her foe, injuring him and destroying his lightsaber.

JEDI MIND TRICK

Now aware that she can use the Force, Rey manages to escape from her cell. Commanding a stormtrooper to release her from the restraint chair, leave the door open and drop his weapon, she is free to reunite with Han and the gang.

CROSSWORD

How much do you know about *Star Wars: The Force Awakens*?

1 1,000 year-old alien from Takodana:

_ _ _   _ _ _ _ _ _

3 Owner of the lightsaber Rey finds in Maz's cantina:

_ _ _ _   _ _ _ _ _ _ _ _ _

9 Name of the super weapon developed by the First Order:

_ _ _ _ _ _ _ _ _ _   _ _ _ _

10 Supreme Leader of the First Order:

_ _ _ _ _

11 Han Solo's loyal co-pilot:

_ _ _ _ _ _ _ _ _

1 Han Solo's trusty ship:

_ _ _ _ _ _ _ _ _ _ _   _ _ _ _ _ _

2 Kylo Ren's grandfather:

_ _ _ _ _   _ _ _ _ _

4 Dark warrior that captures Poe and then Rey:

_ _ _ _   _ _ _

5 Finn's former profession:

_ _ _ _ _ _ _ _ _ _ _ _

6 Name of Chewbacca's weapon:

_ _ _ _ _ _ _ _ _

7 Vicious creatures captured by Han Solo:

_ _ _ _ _ _ _ _

8 Resistance starfighter flown by Poe Dameron:

_ - _ _ _ _

MOVIE MYSTERIES

Some questions left unanswered by *The Force Awakens*

WHO IS REY?

We know that Rey is awaiting the return of her family, but who are they? And with her Force powers self-evident, what is her connection to the Jedi Order and Luke Skywalker in particular?

SKYWALKER SECRETS

After seeing his nephew slaughter his apprentices, Luke apparently goes on a quest to find the first Jedi Temple. Now that he has been located by the Resistance, what will Luke's role be in the ongoing saga? Will he face Kylo Ren and Snoke as the galaxy's last hope?

VADER'S MASK

In *Return of the Jedi* we saw the death of Darth Vader and the ceremonial burning of his body, armour and all. How did Kylo Ren retrieve the damaged mask of his grandfather?

SECRETIVE SNOKE

The Supreme Leader of the First Order seduces a young Kylo Ren to the dark side and promises to complete his training. But who is this shadowy figure and how far has his malevolent influence reached?

FINN'S FUTURE

The former stormtrooper takes on Kylo Ren in a lightsaber battle but is gravely injured. Will he recover from his wounds and resume his role as a key part of the Resistance? Will he fulfil his plans to flee the First Order?

THE FAMOUS WEAPON

Rey experiences terrifying visions when she lays her hands on Luke's lightsaber. But how did the famous weapon find its way into Maz Kanata's castle?

ARE THERE OTHER JEDI?

We are led to believe that Luke is the last surviving Jedi. But with Rey showing incredible Force skills, is she ready to become a Jedi herself?

WILL KYLO REN RETURN?

After Kylo Ren is defeated by Rey, Supreme Leader Snoke promises to complete his apprentice's training. But can the deeply troubled Kylo Ren recover from his physical and mental wounds and become even more powerful?

LIGHTSABER ATTACK

Kylo Ren has sliced up this picture of his father Han Solo. Put the sections in the right order to repair the photo.

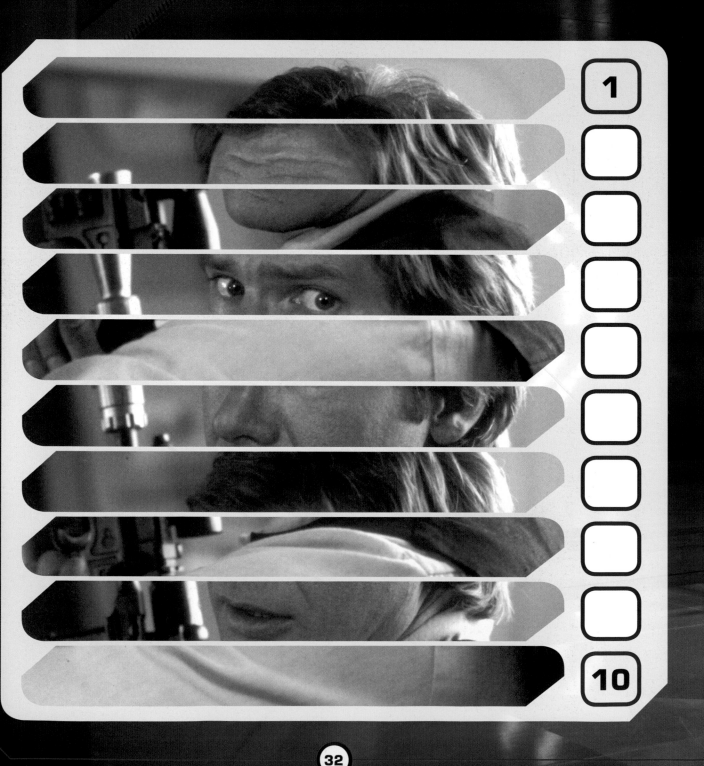

1

10

DROID CLOSE-UPS

Match the droid parts with their owners

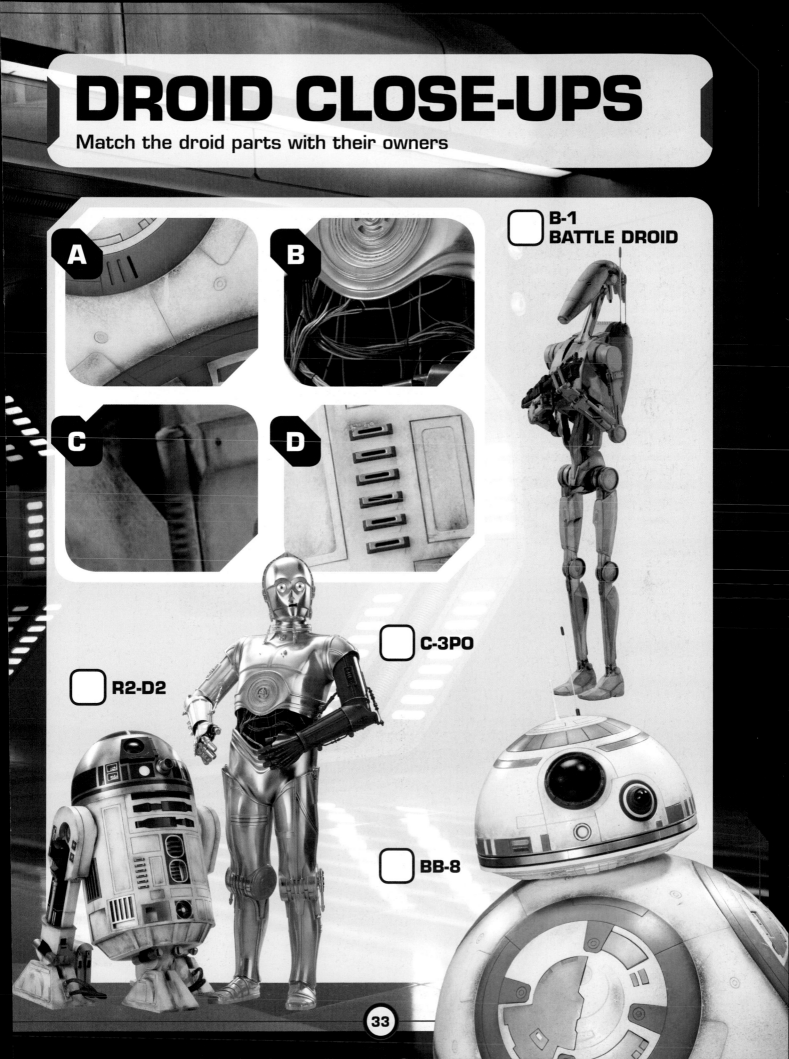

A

B

C

D

B-1
BATTLE DROID

C-3PO

R2-D2

BB-8

RACE TO SAFETY

Negotiate your way through the Outer Rim Territories to the Resistance HQ on D'Qar. But watch out for the First Order!

You will need one counter for each player and a die.

Each player roles a die. The person with the highest number goes first.

Each turn, roll the die and move that number of spaces.

Follow any instructions in the square you land on.

If you land on a square already occupied by a player, move onto the space immediately ahead.

The first person to reach D'Qar wins.

TATOOINE

You need provisions so you take a risk by stopping off at Tatooine. Go back three spaces.

Happy days! On board you win a game of sabacc and receive 200 credits. Move forward one space.

D'QAR

FINISH

START

All clear. Move on two spaces.

You take down a TIE fighter before it can report your location. Go forward a space.

A nightmare beginning to your quest as you are caught in a First Order tractor beam. Go back to the start.

There is a distress call from the Resistance base. Time is short so move on two spaces.

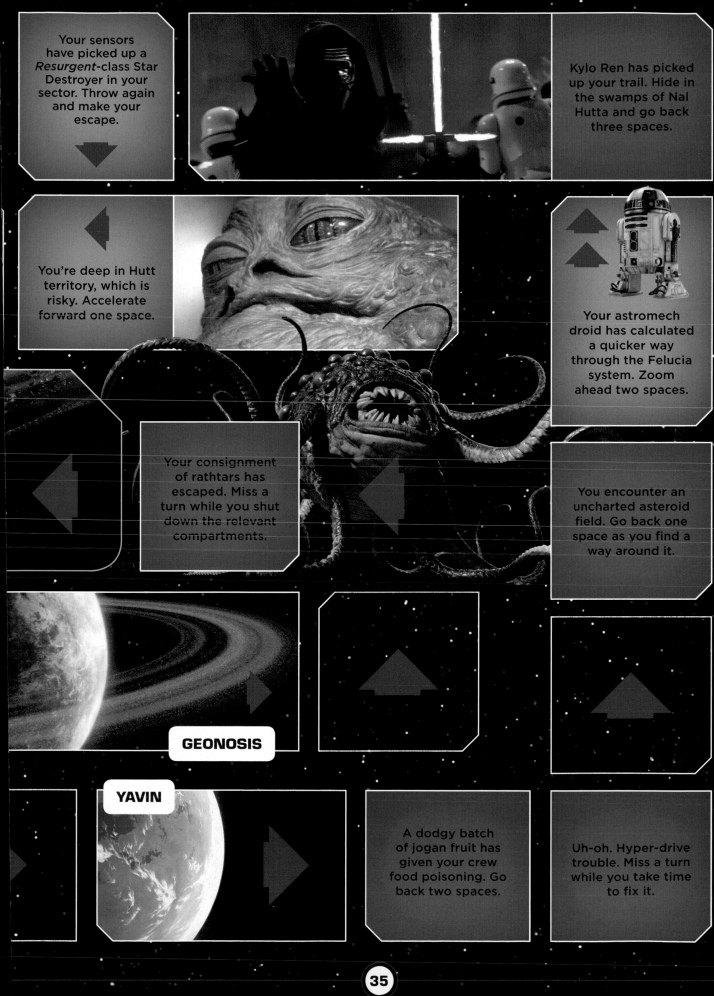

Your sensors have picked up a *Resurgent*-class Star Destroyer in your sector. Throw again and make your escape.

Kylo Ren has picked up your trail. Hide in the swamps of Nal Hutta and go back three spaces.

You're deep in Hutt territory, which is risky. Accelerate forward one space.

Your astromech droid has calculated a quicker way through the Felucia system. Zoom ahead two spaces.

Your consignment of rathtars has escaped. Miss a turn while you shut down the relevant compartments.

You encounter an uncharted asteroid field. Go back one space as you find a way around it.

GEONOSIS

YAVIN

A dodgy batch of jogan fruit has given your crew food poisoning. Go back two spaces.

Uh-oh. Hyper-drive trouble. Miss a turn while you take time to fix it.

TOP VEHICLES
MILLENNIUM FALCON

A closer look at "the fastest hunk of junk in the galaxy"

CREW

A pilot and first mate are ideally required to fly the *Millennium Falcon*, along with gunners to operate the laser cannons. Throughout the ship are also a series of sensor-proof hidden compartments, ideal for smuggling contraband.

DEFENCES

Upgraded over many years, this Corellian YT-1300 light freighter boasts two quad laser cannon turrets, a rotating auto blaster and two racks of concussion missiles, plus electromagnetic counter measures to distract enemy scanners.

DRIVE UNITS

The *Falcon*'s powerful Girodyne sublight drive system can help her reach speeds of up to 1,050 kilometres per hour. While her customised SSP05 hyperdrive is notoriously unreliable, she is one of the fastest ships in the galaxy – Han Solo likes to boast about the time he "made the Kessel Run in less than 12 parsecs."

ARMOUR PLATING

The *Falcon*'s hull is reinforced with titanium plates plus four separate deflector shield generators. These come in very handy when going up against enemy forces or the occasional asteroid field.

SENSOR DISH

The *Falcon*'s sensors allow her crew to spot Imperial ships long before they themselves are detected. Her circular sensor dish was lost during the battle of Endor but 30 years later, by the time of the events of *The Force Awakens*, a rectangular replacement has been installed.

TOP FACTS BB-8

Follow the adventures of this cute and very brave droid

ON THE BALL

BB-8 is an astromech droid with a spherical body on which his head rolls. He is mostly white with orange and silver detailing and a black optical sensor. He also possesses a welding torch and holoprojector.

A LOYAL FRIEND

New Republic Commander Poe Dameron becomes an ally and good friend as they fly together on many missions. Together they visit Jakku to meet Lor San Tekka who hands over a memory drive containing some VERY important information.

SECRET MISSION

On the memory drive is a map revealing the location of missing Jedi Master Luke Skywalker. The First Order want to find and kill him to stop him interfering in their plans, so it is essential the map doesn't fall into enemy hands.

EARY WARNING

Ever on the alert, it is BB-8 who spots approaching First Order Atmospheric Assault Landers. He and Poe try to escape Jakku but their X-wing is attacked by stormtroopers. Poe gives BB-8 the memory drive, urging him to get as far away as possible.

DONE DEAL

On board the *Millennium Falcon*, Finn convinces BB-8 to pretend that the former stormtrooper is actually part of the Resistance. After BB-8 reveals the location of the Resistance base, both exchange a thumbs-up.

ACTION STATIONS

BB-8 flies with Poe as he leads the attack on Starkiller base. After Chewbacca sets off a series of explosions, the squadron of X-wings fire proton torpedoes causing a cataclysmic chain reaction. The battle is over.

UNITED DROIDS

On D'Qar, R2-D2 wakes up at last from his hibernation to reveal an almost-complete map to Luke's location. BB-8 fills in the precious missing piece revealing the exact coordinates of the legendary Jedi Master's hideaway.

FIND LUKE

Using the now completed map, R2-D2, Rey and Chewbacca set out on a mission to find Luke. The map's coordinates lead them to a water world dotted with islands. There, Rey presents Luke with his old lightsaber.

HEAD TO HEAD

Who would win in a showdown between the Zabrak Sith Lord and the Jedi? Give them each scores...

FIGHTING STYLE

Brutally trained by Darth Sidious – later, Emperor Palpatine – as a boy, Maul has a savage hatred for Jedi. He has a relentless, all-action fighting style and is master of lightsaber combat. His Force powers add to his intimidating arsenal.

SCORE /10

INTELLIGENCE

Maul is canny enough to hide all evidence of the Sith during missions of infiltration and assassination. He also had the sheer will to survive being sliced in half by Obi-Wan and return years later during the Clone Wars to take his revenge.

SCORE /10

WEAPONS

Crafted by Maul himself, his primary weapon is a double-bladed lightsaber. It has separate controls so it can be used with a twin or single blade. Each lightsaber also features modulation controls.

SCORE /10

VEHICLE

The Sith Infiltrator, also known as the *Scimitar*, has six laser cannons, surveillance equipment, interrogator droids and contains Maul's speeder bike. An effective cloaking system allows it to travel across the galaxy undetected.

SCORE /10

DARTH MAUL'S SCORE

FIGHTING STYLE

Luke is trained first by Obi-Wan and then Yoda, and shows natural talent for Jedi combat. He loses a duel against the vastly more experienced Vader on Cloud City. However, by the time of the events of *Return of the Jedi*, Luke is more than a match for his father.

SCORE  /10

INTELLIGENCE

Although initially impatient and impetuous, Luke becomes one of the most wise and powerful Jedi ever. His learning and foresight are legendary, although his attempts to steer his nephew Ben from the dark side are ultimately unsuccessful.

SCORE /10

WEAPONS

Luke is proficient in the use of blasters and on-board laser cannons. But like all Jedi, his weapon of choice is a lightsaber, of which he has two. The first is his father's former weapon, the second he builds himself and uses it to defeat Vader in their final battle.

SCORE /10

VEHICLE

A skilled pilot of many crafts, young Skywalker will be forever associated with X-wing starfighters. These are quick and possess four laser cannons and two torpedo launchers. Luke flies an X-wing to destroy the first Death Star.

SCORE /10

LUKE'S SCORE

TOP FACTS
CHEWBACCA
Learn about this legendary Wookiee warrior

NAME:
Chewbacca, or Chewie

SPECIES:
Wookiee

HOME WORLD:
Kashyyyk

JOB:
Co-pilot on the *Millennium Falcon*

WEAPON:
Bowcaster

SPECIAL SKILLS:
Ace pilot, highly skilled mechanic, extraordinary strength, proficient in combat

Following the fall of the Republic, Chewie joins Han Solo on the *Millennium Falcon*. The two make a living doing smuggling jobs for gangsters, including Jabba the Hutt.

Chewbacca encourages the reluctant Han Solo to do the right thing and join the Rebellion. Without their last-minute intervention at the Battle of Yavin, all would have been lost.

After the destruction of the second Death Star, Chewbacca helps free his homeworld Kashyyyk from the Empire.

DRAW CHEWBACCA

Pay tribute to the famous Wookiee by recreating his likeness below

DID YOU KNOW?

Chewbacca is instrumental in the survival of the Jedi Order. Alongside Wookiee chieftain Tarfful, he helps Yoda escape Order 66 after the Battle of Kashyyyk.

Chewbacca is being pursued by bounty hunters and has infiltrated the Death Star!

Can you find him in this busy scene?

When you have found Chewbacca, see if you can spot Han Solo and Boba Fett!

STAR WARS
WHERE'S THE WOOKIEE?

See many more Wookiee hunts in the amazing new activity book *Where's the Wookiee?*

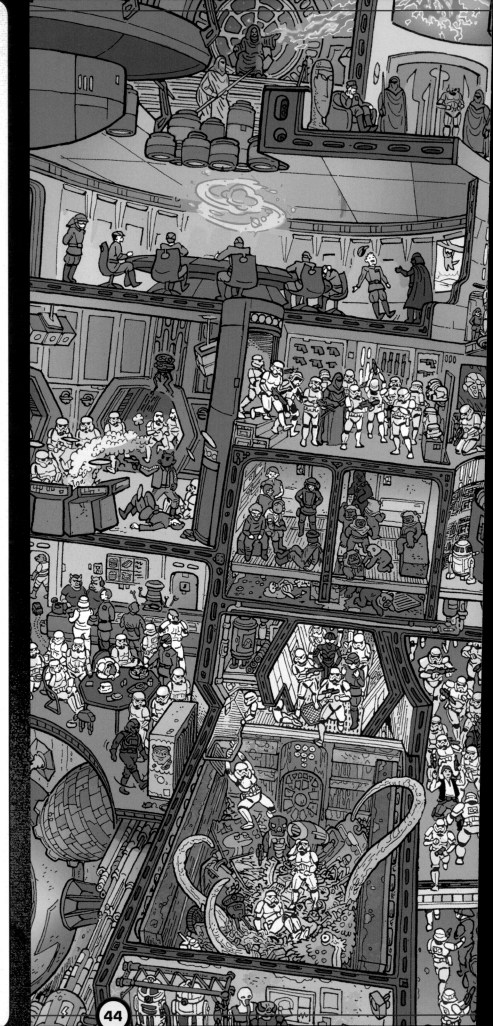

LUKE'S MAP

The map to locate Luke Skywalker is incomplete. Match the fragments to the missing sectors and track down the Jedi

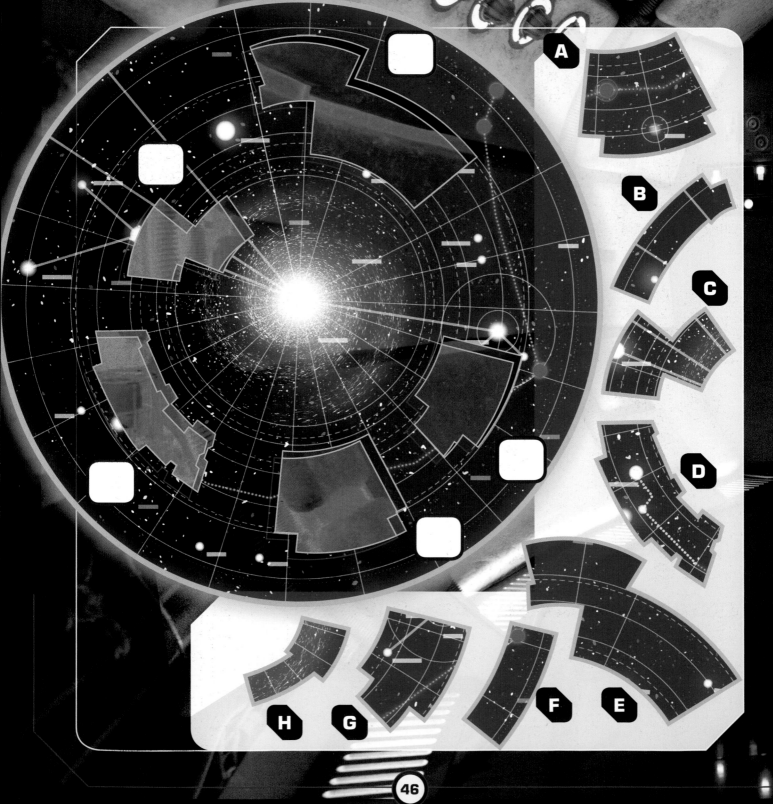

OUT OF THE SHADOWS

Match these *The Force Awakens* characters to their shadows

A   B   C   D

E   F   G   H

☐ POE DAMERON   ☐ FINN   ☐ MAZ KANATA   ☐ CHEWBACCA

☐ REY   ☐ HAN SOLO   ☐ KYLO REN   ☐ CAPTAIN PHASMA

TOP FACTS
HAN SOLO
The finest moments in the life of a heroic smuggler

RESCUING LEIA FROM THE DEATH STAR

After the *Millennium Falcon* was pulled aboard the Death Star by a tractor beam, Han was convinced to help rescue Princess Leia by the vague promise of a reward. Throughout the daring deed, Han and Leia argued continuously but even then we could see that their relationship was one that would endure. Even if it wouldn't always be a smooth ride.

A HERO AT HEART

Thought to have abandoned the Rebels in order to repay his debt to Jabba and ultimately save his skin, Han returned to save the day during the Battle of Yavin. The assault on the Death Star was on the brink of failure, and Vader had Luke's X-wing in his sights. In swooped the *Millennium Falcon*, sending Vader hurtling into space and allowing Luke to destroy the battle station.

RESCUING LUKE (AGAIN)

Attacked by a wampa in the icy Hoth wastelands, Luke was stranded in -60ºC temperatures. Han put aside his plans to leave the planet and found his friend close to death. Cutting open the dead tauntaun, Han shoved Luke inside the carcass before building a shelter that would save both their lives.

HOTH ASTEROID FIELD

Pursued by Star Destroyers after the Battle of Hoth, Han made the decision to navigate through an asteroid belt saying "they'd be crazy to follow us, wouldn't they?" A plan described by C-3PO as having odds of success of "approximately 3,720 to one" did indeed see off his pursuers. The only problem was, he ended up flying right into the mouth of an enormous alien!

HIBERNATION SICKNESS

About to be fed to the hideous sarlacc creature, all seemed lost. Han was temporarily blinded by his time in carbon freezing but still saved Luke by accidentally knocking Boba Fett into the Great Pit of Carkoon. Moments later he freed Lando Calrissian by firing his blaster at the sarlacc, despite being partially sighted.

"CHEWIE, WE'RE HOME"

It was the moment all *Star Wars* fans had been waiting for. Some 30 years after the events of the last movie, Han and Chewie were back aboard their beloved *Millennium Falcon*. Here they teamed up with Rey and Finn, and the search for Luke truly began.

A NOBLE DEATH

Urged by Leia to return their son, Han confronted Kylo Ren on the Starkiller Base. With Ren asking for help to be "free of this pain" and Han saying he would do anything, it seemed that the family would be reunited. Instead, seemingly on the verge of redemption, Ren thrust his lightsaber through Han's chest and our hero fell to his end.

DESTRUCTION OF DEATH STAR II

On the Forest Moon of Endor, Han led a landing party to destroy shield generators protecting the second Death Star. Teaming up with a tribe of Ewoks, Han, Leia, Luke, the droids and some rebel troopers managed to defeat Imperial forces and blow the charges. Alliance ships were able to complete their attack and destroy the battle station.

TOP FACTS
FINN

Check out the amazing journey of this former stormtrooper

EARLY PROMISE

As a cadet, FN-2187 scored top marks in training. Captain Phasma admired his fighting skill but was concerned that he was not ruthless enough in battle.

TRAINED TO DESTROY

Taken as a young boy, Finn is trained by the First Order to be a stormtrooper. He is given the designation FN-2187 and engineered to be an unquestioning fighting machine to serve an evil organisation.

A TURNING POINT

Finn and his fellow troopers are sent to a Jakku village and instructed to execute innocent civilians. Finn, unable to carry out the horrific act, refuses to open fire. He knows he does not belong with the First Order.

A GREAT ESCAPE

Shaken by the events on Jakku, he decides to free the captured Resistance pilot Poe Dameron and steal away from the First Order. Together they take a Special Forces TIE fighter and head towards Jakku.

THE BIRTH OF "FINN"

The duo escapes with some incredible flying from Poe and equally astounding marksmanship from FN-2187. Poe decides that "Finn" would be a much more appropriate name for the former stormtrooper.

SKILLED FIGHTER

Having already shown his fighting prowess in escaping the *Finalizer*, Finn again proves his worth on the *Millennium Falcon*. He teams up with Rey and guns down several TIE fighters in a thrilling dogfight.

THE REVELATION

Finn pretends he is part of the Resistance but later, in Maz Kanata's castle, he confesses he is a stormtrooper. He plans to flee the conflict, afraid of the First Order and their terrifying methods.

RESCUING REY

Abandoning his own selfish interests, Finn offers to be part of the attack on Starkiller Base. He claims to have knowledge of the super weapon's weaknesses in order to free Rey. He captures Captain Phasma and forces her to lower the Starkiller's shield.

FEARLESS SACRIFICE

As the Starkiller Base explodes, Finn engages with Kylo Ren in a lightsaber battle. He fights bravely but suffers grave injuries. Thankfully, Chewbacca pilots the *Millennium Falcon* and rescues Finn before the planet implodes.

HEAD TO HEAD

Who would win in a battle between the Dark Lord of the Sith and the Master Jedi? Give them each scores...

FIGHTING STYLE

Direct, brutal and ruthless, Vader is an intimidating sight. Not only is he an accomplished duelist, he uses his incredible Force powers and immense physical strength to simply overwhelm opponents.

SCORE /10

INTELLIGENCE

Vader is a cunning and hugely experienced warrior and strategist. He leads the pursuit of the rebels across the galaxy, showing he is much more that just the muscle for the evil Empire.

SCORE /10

WEAPONS

Anakin loses his lightsaber during his defeat to Obi-Wan Kenobi, so Darth Vader must build another one to better match his new calling. He constructs a darker alloy weapon and uses a red kyber crystal to give it its distinctive blade.

SCORE /10

VEHICLE

Vader flew the TIE Advanced X1, a faster and sleeker version of the standard TIE fighters. It possessed a hyperdrive and deflector shield generator, plus fixed-mounted twin blaster cannons and cluster missiles.

SCORE /10

DARTH VADER'S SCORE

FIGHTING STYLE

Having trained Jedi for hundreds of years, Yoda has perfected the art of fighting. He wields a lightsaber as if it were an extension of his own body. He can deflect Force lightning and manipulate objects.

SCORE /10

INTELLIGENCE

Yoda's wisdom is legendary and as Grand Master of the Jedi council he leads this mystical order with dignity and great judgement. But even with his great powers of perception, Yoda is unable to detect Chancellor Palpatine's evil agenda.

SCORE /10

WEAPONS

Yoda's lightsaber has a shorter blade and reduced hilt to match its owner's size. This green-bladed weapon stays with him throughout the Clone Wars until he loses it fighting Palpatine in the Senate Chamber.

SCORE /10

VEHICLE

During the Clone Wars he uses a modified starfighter to embark on a mission to Dagobah. Although smaller than standard starfighters, it still has space for an astromech droid, and R2-D2 accompanies Yoda on this adventure.

SCORE /10

YODA'S SCORE

FEEL THE FORCE

Used for good or evil, here's a run-down of the greatest Force powers

1 MOVING OBJECTS

Yoda raises Luke's X-wing from the Dagobah swamp in an iconic moment, but nothing can match the drama of when Obi-Wan summons Qui-Gon's lightsaber to cut down Darth Maul.

2 INFLICTING PAIN

Kylo Ren extracts information from Poe Dameron by using his Force powers. Darth Vader often administers fatal punishment when he is displeased, using only his mind to choke his luckless victims.

3 MIND CONTROL

On Tatooine, Obi-Wan is able to wrong-foot stormtroopers searching for our heroes. The suggestion "these are not the droids you are looking for" was enough to deceive the bad guys.

2. REPELLING OPPONENTS

Force-sensitive individuals can dismiss adversaries with a thought. Master Yoda demonstrates this technique when he confronts Emperor Palpatine.

OBI-WAN KENOBI

5

PHYSICAL AGILITY

Whilst Jedi and Sith use the power of the mind first and foremost, both boast incredible physical advantages. Darth Maul's acrobatics against Obi-Wan and Qui-Gon plus Luke's leap from the carbonite chamber on Cloud City are classic examples.

6 GOING BEYOND DEATH

The wisest Jedi are able to transcend death by living on as Force spirits. At the end of the *Return of the Jedi*, Luke sees Obi-Wan, Yoda and his redeemed father, Anakin in their new ghost-like forms.

7 SENSING FAR-OFF EMOTIONS

After discovering that Darth Vader is his father, Luke is defeated and needs to be rescued. His sister Leia is able to sense his mental cry for help and rescues him in the *Millennium Falcon*.

8

FORCE LIGHTNING

Force lightning is used by powerful exponents of the dark side. The ability to cast lightning from the tips of one's fingers is a powerful weapon, although one that ultimately left Darth Sidious scarred.

9 SENSING DEATH

Obi-Wan instinctively feels when the people of Alderaan are destroyed by the Death Star. Later, Leia senses when Han meets his end at the hands of their estranged son Kylo Ren.

10 SEEING THE FUTURE

Anakin's visions of his mother's death and then later the demise of his wife Padmé come true – but these are only possible futures. As Yoda says, "Always in motion is the future."

SAY WHAT?

Match the famous *Star Wars* quotes to their characters

1 "We meet again, at last. The circle is now complete. When I left you, I was but the learner; now I am the master."

2 "I was raised to do one thing... but I've got nothing to fight for."

3 "Show me again the power of the darkness, and I'll let nothing stand in our way. Show me, grandfather, and I will finish what you started."

4 "Chewie, we're home."

5 "If you see our son, bring him home."

6 "You will remove these restraints and leave this cell with the door open."

7 "When 900 years old, you reach, look as good, you will not."

8 "You were the chosen one! It was said that you would destroy the Sith, not join them."

9 "The Force is strong with you. A powerful Sith you will become. Henceforth, you shall be known as Darth... Vader."

10 "Sir, the possibility of successfully navigating an asteroid field is approximately 3,720 to 1."

A C-3PO

B REY

C HAN SOLO

D DARTH VADER

E KYLO REN

F DARTH SIDIOUS

G LEIA ORGANA

H FINN

I OBI-WAN KENOBI

J YODA

© 2016 LFL

ANSWERS

P12 – GREAT ESCAPE

P14 – SECRET WEAPON
STARKILLER BASE

P22 – TROOPER TROUBLE

P23 – BB-8 SEARCH

V	L	V	F	A	L	C	O	N	C	J	Q	M	C	H
Z	G	R	E	S	I	S	T	A	N	C	E	H	D	G
Y	L	E	Y	D	B	E	P	P	N	A	R	T	O	O
L	E	P	C	H	E	W	B	A	C	C	A	R	Y	G
E	I	U	G	L	D	O	M	G	K	J	K	E	J	M
F	A	B	M	R	F	L	I	Y	J	Y	R	G	K	A
G	O	L	K	A	H	K	L	A	N	H	X	Q	R	Z
N	R	I	M	Y	F	O	K	O	F	Q	N	U	A	K
N	G	C	K	R	R	K	G	O	P	V	M	K	Z	A
I	A	Z	U	E	U	S	X	T	I	X	P	X	D	N
F	N	S	N	O	R	E	M	A	D	E	O	P	H	A
D	A	U	N	K	A	R	P	L	U	T	T	G	H	T
T	K	G	D	I	Q	Z	O	L	O	S	N	A	H	A
H	C	B	Q	R	E	D	R	O	T	S	R	I	F	U
S	T	A	R	K	I	L	L	E	R	I	S	Q	K	V

P26 – CROSSWORD

ACROSS
1 Maz Kanata, 3 Luke Skywalker, 9 Starkiller
Base, 10 Snoke, 11 Chewbacca

DOWN
1 *Millennium Falcon*, 2 Darth Vader, 3 Kylo Ren
5 Stormtrooper, 6 Bowcaster, 7 Rathtars
8 X-wing

P32 – LIGHTSABER ATTACK
1, 3, 7, 4, 9, 5, 2, 8, 6, 10

P33 – DROID CLOSE-UPS
A – BB-8
B – C-3PO
C – B-1 BATTLE DROID
D – R2-D2

P46 – LUKE'S MAP
CLOCKWISE FROM TOP
E, G, A, D, C

P47 – OUT OF THE SHADOWS
A Rey, B Maz Kanata, C Finn, D Kylo Ren,
E Chewbacca, F Poe Dameron, G Han Solo,
H Captain Phasma

P58 – SAY WHAT?
1-D, 2-H, 3-E, 4-C, 5-G, 6-B, 7-J, 8-I, 9-F, 10-A

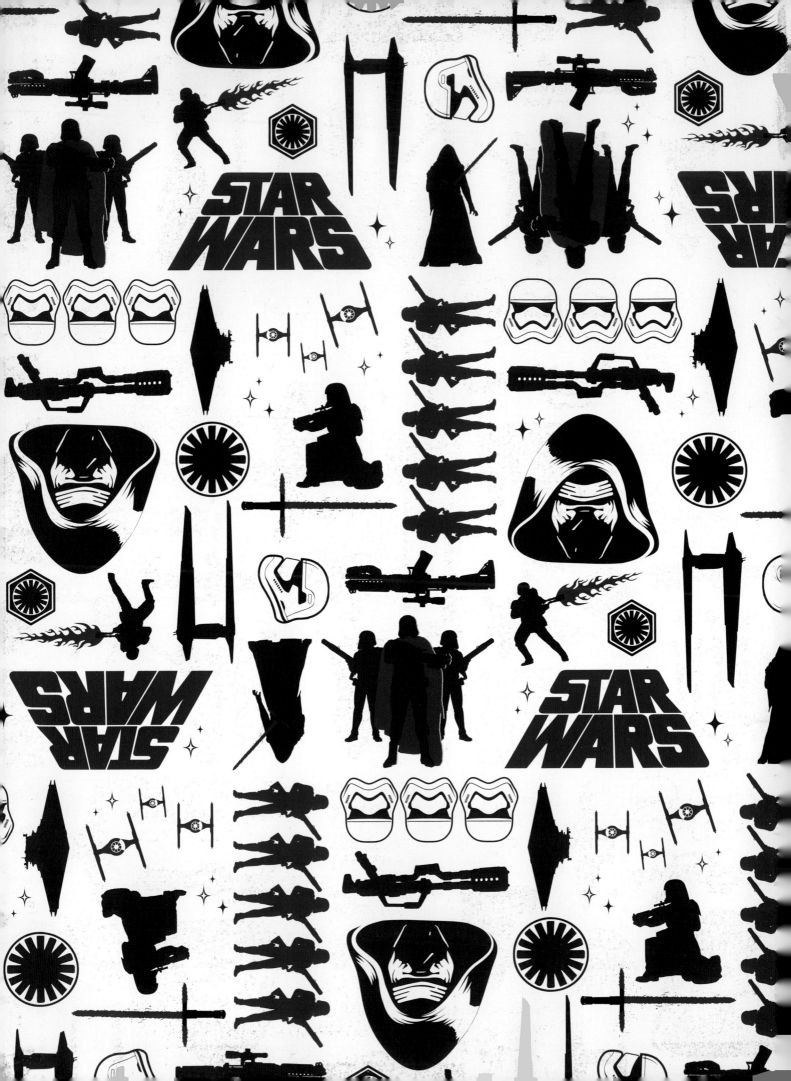